# PLANNING ISN'T MY PRIORITY...

# AND MAKING PRIORITIES ISN'T IN MY PLANS!

NOW!

Later

Published by

**National Center for Youth Issues**

Practical Guidance Resources
Educators Can Trust

ncyi.org

www.ncyi.org

To Courtney - the Master Planner

Love, Mom

## Duplication and Copyright

**National Center for Youth Issues**
Practical Guidance Resources
Educators Can Trust
ncyi.org

P.O. Box 22185
Chattanooga, TN 37422-2185
423.899.5714 • 866.318.6294
fax: 423.899.4547 • www.ncyi.org

ISBN: 978-1-937870-39-3    Retail US: $9.95
© 2017 National Center for Youth Issues, Chattanooga, TN
All rights reserved.
Written by: Julia Cook
Illustrations by: Michelle Hazelwood Hyde
Design by: Phillip W. Rodgers
Contributing Editor: Beth Spencer Rabon
Published by National Center for Youth Issues • Softcover
Printed at Starkey Printing, Chattanooga, Tennessee, U.S.A., May 2017

My name is Cletus.

Sometimes, I have a hard time planning stuff out.

It's hard for me to figure out what needs to be done first,

and I don't like to think about what I have to do next.

I just like to **"LIVE IN THE MOMENT!"**

*I know there's a NOW and a LATER,*

*but I'd rather just think about NOW.*

*Planning just isn't my priority.*

*And setting priorities???*

*I don't even know how!*

"Cletus! You mean to tell me that we hiked all the way up here to camp, and you forgot the tent?"

"OOOOPS."

"Cletus...you needed to put the chips in the cookie dough **before** you baked the cookies!"

"I forgot."

"Cletus... Where is your swimsuit?"

"I didn't plan on going swimming."

4

"Cletus!!! It's 10pm!

What do you mean you don't have your homework done yet? What have you been doing?

Cletus, you need to have a *plan*, and set better *priorities*!!

Why can't you be more like Bocephus? That's how you should be!!!"

5

Bocephus is my cousin.

He's a MASTER PLANNER!

He plans every minute of every day of his life!

It wouldn't surprise me if Bocephus had a plan for when to

BREATHE!!!

6

Bocephus always tells me:

"If you want to do well in life, you need to get your *priorities* straight.

You must make a *plan* to get everything done.

At *planning*, Cletus... you're not so great!"

But if anything ever happens to mess up Bocephus' plans...

He totally LOSES IT!!!

Schedule Monday
6:00 - wake
6:05 Brush t...
6:15 Dress
7:00 Breakfast
7:30 Leave for School

This year, Bocephus and I are partners for the science fair, so we decided to do our project on mealworms.

Bocephus *planned* to buy the mealworms, and his *plan* for me was to develop a hypothesis for our project...

whatever **that** is.

Today my teacher asked me...

**"Cletus, what is your hypothesis?"**

**"My** h~y~wh^a^t^t^**a?"**

I looked over at Bocephus. He just about lost it!
Then he gave me the unibrow and said...

"We hypothesize that mealworms
will prefer a warm, dry climate
with lots of light as opposed to a
damp, dim, cooler climate."

"Excellent!"

my teacher said.

On the way home from school Bocephus said...

**"Why didn't you stick to the plan, Cletus?
You knew what you needed to do!"**

**"I forgot, I said. Besides, I was busy
with scissors and paper and glue!"**

**"Doing what?"**

**"I made an
obstacle course
for the mealworms!!!**

**It has a slide and
steps and a tunnel!**

**There's a maze and
a pool to swim in!**

**And you should see
what I did with a
funnel!!!"**

# "Cletus!

*Planning* is a thinking skill that helps us develop strategies to accomplish our goal. Our goal is to **WIN** the science fair, not give our mealworms the vacation of a lifetime!

## STICK TO THE PLAN!!!"

Then Bocephus handed me the mealworms and said...

*"My mom doesn't allow bugs in the house, so these have to go home with you.*

*I'll practice my banjo, do homework and eat dinner, then I'll come over at* 6:32 .

*Mealworms eat bran flakes, so keep them in here. But make sure you keep the box shut.*

*And keep this box away from the kitchen... so they don't end up in somebody's gut!"*

(Bocephus knows that both me and my dad LOVE, LOVE, LOVE bran flakes.)

At 6:32, Bocephus came over...but I wasn't home. I sorta forgot that we were doing our science fair stuff, and I'd gone to get ice cream with my dad.

Bocephus **TOTALLY** lost it, gave my mom the unibrow, and stomped all the way back to his house.

"I can't work with Cletus! he said to his mom.
He doesn't follow the plan...

He's the most uNOrganIZEd person that I've ever known!
I can't do this Mom...

I just CAN'T!!!"

"HIS plan or YOURS Bocephus? Did you agree on what to do?
Or did you just tell Cletus, and expect him to follow through?"

*"You can't plan the lives of others and expect them to do what you say. You should be more like Cletus, and put flexibility into your day!*

*You and Cletus should come up with a plan, so that both of you agree on what to do and how to do it. Then you will be more stress free."*

When I got home, Bocephus
came back over.

"Cletus…we need to talk!" he said.

"I'm sorry for getting mad at you,
because you didn't follow my *plan*.

I guess I should be more *flexible*,
and if I try, I think that I can."

But Cletus, you
should try harder
to *prioritize* your life.

I think I know
how to help you,
if you will
give it a try."

18

# "Setting *priorities* is easy.

Just write down what needs to be done.

Then number your list
from first to last,
and start with your number one! #1

Then think about what will happen,
if you don't spend the time that you need.

You must learn the difference between
your NEEDS and your WANTS.

If you don't, you won't succeed."

*"Every time you play a video game, you make a plan inside your head.*

*You develop long and short-term goals, and you remember what you've read.*

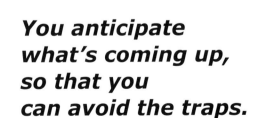

*You anticipate what's coming up, so that you can avoid the traps.*

*You set priorities on what to do first, and you remember what to do last."*

21

"You learn from mistakes
and use what you learn,
so you don't make
those mistakes again.

Every time you play a video game,
you *plan* and *prioritize* to **WIN!**"

"I never thought about it like that," I said.

Bocephus was right! I was planning and prioritizing every day, and I didn't even know it!!

And, based on my video game scores, I might even be better at it than **he** is!!!!

CLETUS

Bocephus and I sat down together, and we wrote out a new science fair project *plan*.

**#1** **First,** we wrote down the big things that we needed to do.

Then, we decided who would do **what** and **when**.

We talked about what would happen if we didn't get the stuff on our lists done, and we talked about all the stuff that could go wrong, and what to do about it.

Bocephus even agreed to use my **obstacle course** to collect our data!

Then we went into my room to get started.

I had accidentally left the bran flakes box open, and our mealworms had escaped!

**They were EVERYWHERE in my room!!!**

"OOOPS!
          **We didn't plan on this!"**

I looked at Bocephus.
I thought for sure he'd lose it...
but he didn't.

He didn't even make a unibrow!

All he said was, "I'm sure glad this didn't happen at my house! My mom would have totally lost it!"

(Maybe it runs in the family.)

We gathered up all of the mealworms,
and used the *plan* inside our heads.

We met our long and short-term goals,
and we remembered what we had read.

We anticipated what might happen,
so we could avoid the traps.

We set our *priorities* of what
to do first, and
we remembered
what to do last.

We made some mistakes,
but we used what we learned
so we wouldn't make them again.

**Planning** and **prioritizing** really paid off,
because we ended up with a **WIN!**"

# Tips For Teaching Kids to Plan and Prioritize

Planning and prioritizing are two of the most difficult executive function skills for people to master. Planning effectively is the thinking skill that helps an individual develop strategies to accomplish goals. It allows a person to think about completing a task before it is started. Life is all about making choices, and prioritizing effectively helps a person make the best choices possible. Time is a limited commodity, and to get the most out of your time and accomplish all that you need to do, you have to be able to plan and prioritize both on a long and short-term basis.

Here are a few tips that you might find helpful when teaching kids how to plan and prioritize their lives.

- Think about your overall plan…What is your ultimate goal?

- Make a list of everything that needs to be done to accomplish your goal. What needs to happen? What supplies will you need?

- Put your list in order. Think about what is urgent.  What needs to be done **NOW**, and what can be done **LATER**?

- Determine the differences between your **NEEDS** and your **WANTS**.

- Decide what things on your list are **BIG** things (family responsibilities, getting good grades, etc.) and what things are **SMALL** things (getting that new video game that just came out.)  Things that may seem very important to you now may not be quite as important to you a few weeks or months from now.

- Think about the consequences involved if you don't get the stuff on your list done. What would happen if you played your video game instead of doing your math homework? What would happen if you didn't turn in your science report, etc?

- Anticipate things that might go wrong, and make a plan for what to do if that happens.

- When you make a mistake, learn from it, and do your best not to make that same mistake again in the future.

Sometimes there is not enough time to do all that you want to do, and you have to make a choice because you just can't do everything.  When this happens, and you don't know what to do, ask yourself the following questions:

**1.** What do these things mean to me? If I have to give something up, which thing will I miss the most? Which one will I miss the least?

**2.** Is this a **NOW OR NEVER** situation? Will I have another chance to do this in the future?

**3.** Am I doing this for me or to please someone else?

In order to succeed in our busy world, children must learn how to plan and set priorities.

Always remember that Benjamin Franklin said it best,

## *"If you fail to plan, you are planning to fail!"*

- **Benjamin Franklin**